The Great Railway Show

Illustrated by Tommy Stubbs

A Random House PICTUREBACK® Book

Random House 🏠 New York

Thomas the Tank Engine & Friends™

CREATED BY BRITT ALLCROFT

Based on the Railway Series by the Reverend W Awdry.
© 2016 Gullane (Thomas) LLC. Thomas the Tank Engine & Friends and Thomas & Friends are trademarks of Gullane (Thomas) Limited.
Thomas the Tank Engine & Friends and Design Is Reg. U.S. Pat. & Tm. Off. © 2016 HIT Entertainment Limited.
HIT and the HIT Entertainment logo are trademarks of HIT Entertainment Limited.
All rights reserved. Published in the United States by Random House Children's Books, a division of Penguin Random House LLC, 1745
Broadway, New York, NY 10019, and in Canada by Penguin Random House Canada Limited, Toronto. Pictureback, Random House, and
the Random House colophon are registered trademarks of Penguin Random House LLC.
randomhousekids.com   www.thomasandfriends.com
ISBN 978-1-101-93202-5 (trade) — ISBN 978-1-101-93203-2 (ebook)
Printed in the United States of America
10 9 8 7 6 5 4 3 2

One sunny day on the Island of Sodor, Thomas the Tank Engine saw a shiny new engine in Vicarstown Station.

"That's my brother, the Flying Scotsman," Gordon said with a sigh.

The Flying Scotsman was going to the Great Railway Show on the Mainland. "That's where engines compete to see who's fastest and strongest," he explained.

Thomas was excited. He wanted to go, too!

Thomas thought that if some streamlining could be added to an engine from Sodor, it could win races at the show.

"What an excellent idea!" said Sir Topham Hatt. "We'll streamline Gordon and he'll be faster than ever!"

Gordon! That was *not* what Thomas had in mind!

The next day a railway ferry delivered engines from all over the world to Brendam Docks.

"Where are you going?" the Dock Manager asked.

"The Great Railway Show," puffed a streamlined engine from Belgium.

"That'll be on the Mainland," the Manager replied.

The engines jostled and pushed past Thomas as they got back on the ferry.

Rushing for the departing ferry, a brightly painted engine named Ashima bumped into Thomas.

"Whoa!" he peeped as he teetered on the edge of the quay.

Dockworkers quickly wrapped a chain around Thomas' coupling hook. Ashima helped pull him to safety.

Ashima apologized to Thomas and asked about another way to get to the Mainland.

Thomas didn't answer. He just chugged away in a huff.

"Why should *she* get to go to the Great Railway Show?" Thomas puffed.

"Well, she's very beautifully painted," Clarabel said.

That gave Thomas an idea. Off he sped to the Steamworks.

Thomas asked Victor to repaint him with lightning bolts and racing stripes.

Just then, Sir Topham Hatt came by to check on Gordon's streamlining. He liked the idea of a speedy-looking paint job— but not for Thomas.

Meanwhile, over at the Dieselworks, Diesel had his own idea. He wanted to disguise Paxton, Den, and Dart as trucks and pretend to pull them.

"It'll look like I'm pulling a very heavy train by myself," he said, snickering. "If Sir Topham Hatt thinks I'm stronger than Henry, he'll take me to the Great Railway Show instead."

Later that day, Thomas met Ashima again. She didn't understand why Thomas had wanted to be repainted.

"You can only be you," she tooted. "Every engine I've ever known was useful and had a job to do." Ashima asked if Thomas was good at shunting and sorting trucks.

"Yes," Thomas peeped. And then he had his best idea yet for going to the Great Railway Show. "I'll show Sir Topham Hatt what *I* can do best!"

The next day, Thomas went to practice his shunting at Knapford Station. The rails were blocked by Diesel's tricky trucks, so Thomas decided to move them.

"What are you doing?" Diesel hissed. "You'll spoil my trick!"

Thomas began to pull the disguised Diesels. He was surprised by how easily and fast everything moved!

He tried to stop at a red signal ahead, but the Diesels kept pushing because they couldn't hear the warning bell.

CRASH! Thomas collided with a passing engine!

Now what will happen? Is Thomas all right? Will he go to the Great Railway Show? And if he does, what will happen there?

To find out, turn this book over and right-side up—and begin reading.

Sir Topham Hatt was proud of Thomas for being Really Useful—
and very thoughtful, too.

"He was just being himself, Sir!" peeped Percy.
"You can only be you," Thomas puffed. He winked at Ashima. "There's
nothing else you can possibly do."

A little while later, everyone gathered for the award ceremony. "We would like to declare *two* winners in the Shunting Challenge," a judge announced. "Ashima wins for the fastest time, and Thomas also wins—for helping his competitor."

The two engines steamed back and forth, buffering boxcars into place. Soon their sidings were full. Now it was a race to the finish line. Then Thomas noticed an overturned truck on Ashima's track! He sped up to push it out of her way.

Ashima raced to victory.

Thomas chuffed through round after round, pulling tankers and flatbeds into line. He did better than engines from Russia, Italy, and Brazil.

In the end, there were only two engines left—Thomas and Ashima!

A whistle blew and the final challenge began.

Meanwhile, over at the Shunting Challenge, Percy was too scared to enter the race. He wanted Thomas to compete in his place—which had been the original plan.

"Okay," Thomas peeped. "But I might not win, you know."

Gordon sped down the tracks. "Shooting Star coming through!" he tooted. Suddenly his face turned red. Steam hissed from inside his streamlining.

Gordon's brother, the Flying Scotsman, told him something was wrong, but Gordon wouldn't listen. Then his boiler burst! He sputtered to a stop in a cloud of steam as the other engines raced past.

Victor soon discovered that Gordon's safety valve hadn't been installed after his streamlining! Without it, he could overheat during his race.

Even though his own repairs weren't done, Thomas took the valve to Gordon.

At the Great Railway Show, Thomas found Gordon at the starting line of the Great Race.

Gordon didn't believe that the Steamworks team had made a mistake. And the race was starting!

A whistle blew and the engines were off!

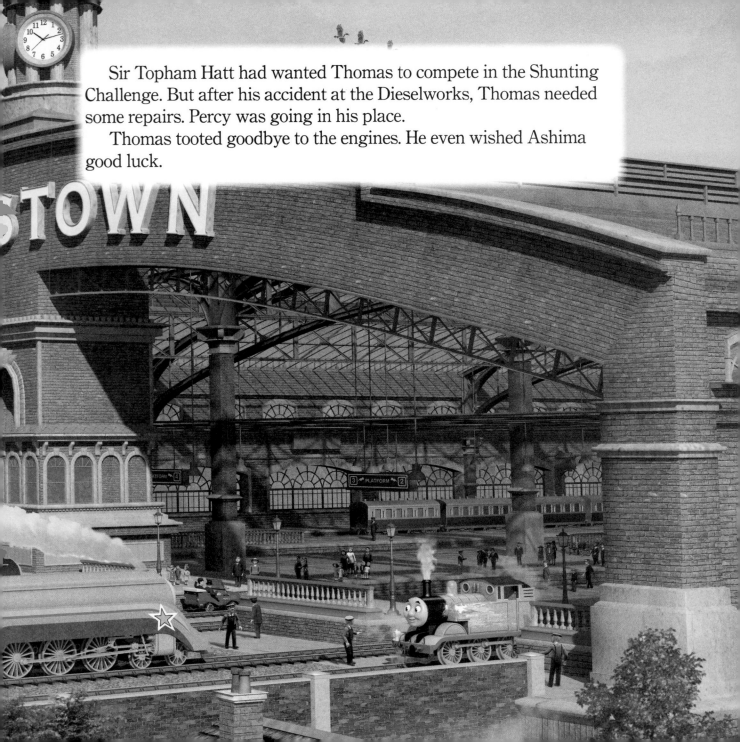

Sir Topham Hatt had wanted Thomas to compete in the Shunting Challenge. But after his accident at the Dieselworks, Thomas needed some repairs. Percy was going in his place.

Thomas tooted goodbye to the engines. He even wished Ashima good luck.

It was the day of the Great Railway Show. All the engines on Sodor were excited. The engines Sir Topham Hatt had chosen were ready to go. Gordon had been painted and streamlined. He even had a new nameplate: The Shooting Star.

Off to the Races!

Illustrated by Tommy Stubbs

A Random House PICTUREBACK® Book

Random House 🏠 New York

Thomas the Tank Engine & Friends™

CREATED BY BRITT ALLCROFT

Based on the Railway Series by the Reverend W Awdry.
© 2016 Gullane (Thomas) LLC. Thomas the Tank Engine & Friends and Thomas & Friends are trademarks of Gullane (Thomas) Limited. Thomas the Tank Engine & Friends and Design Is Reg. U.S. Pat. & Tm. Off. © 2016 HIT Entertainment Limited.
HIT and the HIT Entertainment logo are trademarks of HIT Entertainment Limited.
All rights reserved. Published in the United States by Random House Children's Books, a division of Penguin Random House LLC, 1745 Broadway, New York, NY 10019, and in Canada by Penguin Random House Canada Limited, Toronto. Pictureback, Random House, and the Random House colophon are registered trademarks of Penguin Random House LLC.
randomhousekids.com   www.thomasandfriends.com
ISBN 978-1-101-93202-5 (trade) — ISBN 978-1-101-93203-2 (ebook)
Printed in the United States of America
10 9 8 7 6 5 4 3 2